Great Expectations

Retold by
Mary Sebag-Montefiore

Illustrated by Barry Ablett

Reading Consultant: Alison Kelly
Roehampton University

Contents

Chapter 1

The man in the mist

The churchyard was damp and overgrown. I crouched among the nettles, by the graves of my father, my mother and my little brothers. The wind roared around me and twenty miles away, across the marsh, the sea howled. Mist and fog waved long white fingers through the churchyard. "Death has stolen everyone I loved," I thought, and began to cry.

"Stop that noise, you little devil, or I'll cut your throat!"

A hand suddenly grabbed my shoulder, and, turning, I saw a man burst through the mist into view — a terrible wild-haired man. His clothes were wet, torn and smothered in mud; his shoes were worn through, his teeth chattered. Locked on his legs was a chain that dragged and clanged as he shook me fiercely.

"Don't hurt me! Please!" I begged,
in terror.

"What's your name, boy?" he growled.
"Quick!"

"Pip, Sir."

"Where do you live, Pip?" He gripped
my wrists.

"Down there, Sir," I nodded. "Past the
church. With Joe, the
blacksmith, and his
wife. That's my
sister, Sir."

"Blacksmith, eh?" He pushed me down
onto a tombstone, so that his eyes
beamed down on mine, and mine looked
helplessly up at his.

"You know what a file is, Pip?" he asked.

"Y-Yes, Sir. It's a saw that goes through iron."

"Get me one, first thing in the morning. Get me food, too, or I'll rip your heart and liver out. Don't think you're safe. I know where you live."

"I-I w-w-will," I stammered.

"Swear it. Say Lord strike you dead if you don't."

I said it, and he let go of me. Terrified, I ran home, fast, turning just once to see him jump over the churchyard wall and disappear into the empty black marsh.

My sister met me with a broomstick, which she whacked against my bottom.

"Curse the boy!" she yelled. "Late again. No supper for you!"

As she spoke, a loud BANG! exploded in my ears, like a huge gun.

"What's that?" I cried.

"The police," said my sister, grimly.

"What are they doing?"

"They're firing to warn of an escaped prisoner from the Hulk."

"Please, what's the Hulk?" I asked.

My sister shook me. "Where you'll end up if you don't stop asking questions. It's a prison-ship for bad people, like murderers and robbers." She pushed me with the end of the broomstick. "Go up to bed. Now!"

I didn't starve that night because kind Joe crept up secretly with some supper for me. But my dreams were haunted by an evil villain with clanking chains, and I kept waking, terrified he'd come for me.

At dawn I went down, took Joe's file from his forge – I knew he wouldn't mind once he understood – and stole a big pork pie and a bottle of brandy from the kitchen. My sister, unlike Joe, would be furious when she discovered the theft, and I prayed she wouldn't guess the thief was me.

Chapter 2

The strange bride

The man was waiting for me by the churchyard. "Bless you, boy," he grunted, seizing the stuff from my hands. He gulped the brandy and tore sharp, snapping bites off the pie, like a dog.

Then he grabbed the file and began sawing at his chain, his eyes shifting sideways as if expecting danger from everywhere.

"I shan't forget you, boy," he said. "Remember me. Abel Magwitch, that's my name."

"I won't forget you, Sir," I said. I meant it. I knew he'd disturb my thoughts forever. He was still sawing as I ran back home over the marsh.

Inside, I found Joe and my sister with a visitor, Mr. Jaggers, the lawyer. He looked me up and down through his bushy eyebrows, like a judge. I thought my sister had summoned him because I was a thief and I shook in my shoes.

"You're lucky, Pip," Joe put in, relieving my fears.

"You should be grateful," my sister interrupted. "Mr. Jaggers says Miss Havisham wants you to visit her. Today."

I was stunned. Miss Havisham was a rich old woman who lived in a large house in our village and never saw anyone.

My sister washed my face and hair, kneading her hands into my scalp until I saw stars. But no matter how many questions I asked, she couldn't throw light on why Miss Havisham wanted me.

Mr. Jaggers and I arrived at Miss Havisham's gate. Behind was an overgrown courtyard.

Mr. Jaggers, swelling with importance, jangled the bell and a very pretty, haughty-looking girl arrived.

"You must be Pip," she said, looking at me. Then she turned to Mr. Jaggers. "Do you want to see Miss Havisham?" she asked.

"If she wants to see me," replied Mr. Jaggers, expectantly.

"She doesn't," said the girl. Then she pulled me through the gate and closed it, leaving Mr. Jaggers staring after us.

In we went. All the passages were dark. At last we stopped outside a large, oak door.

"Go in," she ordered.

"After you," I said, more in shyness than politeness.

"Don't be ridiculous," she replied, walking away. "I'm not going in."

Half-afraid, I pushed open the door and found myself in a large room, well-lit with wax candles, but without a drop of daylight. Seated in a chair, her elbow on a table, her head resting on her hand, was the strangest lady I had ever seen.

She wore white, like a bride. A long white veil hung from her head, and even her hair was white. Then I realized that all the things I thought were white were faded and yellow. The flowers in her hair were dead and withered, and the bride within the dress was old and withered too.

The table, laid for a feast, was hung with cobwebs that draped over the candlesticks. Towering over them, like a black fungus, was an ancient wedding cake. I could see spiders scurrying in and out.

"Look at me," she said, turning her sunken eyes to me. "Are you afraid of a woman who has not seen the sun since before you were born?"

"No," I lied.

"Do you know what I touch here?" she asked, laying one hand upon the other on her left side.

"Your heart, ma'am?" I queried.

"Broken!" she said eagerly, smiling a strange smile that had a kind of boast in it. "I am tired," she went on. "I want to see a child play. So play! Play!"

I couldn't. I didn't know what to do.

"Are you sulking? Are you obstinate?" she demanded.

"N-No," I stammered.

"Call Estella," she ordered.

To shout for the snooty girl was as bad as being told to play. But I did, and she came down the dark corridor with a candle.

"Play," insisted Miss Havisham.

Estella looked horrified. "With this common, clumsy boy?"

"Well," she murmured, "you can break his heart." I couldn't believe my ears. It seemed such a strange and terrible thing to say.

We played cards until Estella won.

"Come here!" ordered Miss Havisham, beckoning me over. "Do you think she's pretty?" she asked in a whisper.

"Yes," I whispered back. "But she's very insulting."

"Hah!" I think she looked pleased. "Go now, Pip. Come again next week."

Estella led me back to the gate. Just as I was leaving, she smiled at me, tilting her face up to mine. "So you think I'm pretty?" she asked.

"Very pretty," I said.

"Am I still insulting?" she asked softly.

"Not as much as when I arrived," I replied.

"No?" she responded, and slapped my face with all the strength she had.

"What do you think of me now, you foul little monster?"

I refused to answer.

Chapter 3

Lucky lad

Back home, my sister and Joe were curious, but I didn't feel like telling them anything.

"You behave properly, and she might leave you her fortune," said my sister.

"Pip doesn't need a fortune; he's got a good home here," Joe smiled. "He'll be a blacksmith, just like me."

I sighed. I didn't want to be a blacksmith, like Joe. I wanted to be rich, so that Estella wouldn't despise me.

Week after week, year after year, I went to Miss Havisham's house to play with Estella. Nothing ever changed. Wearing her crumbling bride clothes, Miss Havisham stayed indoors, watching over us with her strange smile.

At last the time came when Joe said I was old enough to start work as his apprentice. My dream of being a rich gentleman was at an end. My sister had died suddenly of a fever. I felt I couldn't leave Joe, now he was on his own. I'd have to be a workman, just like him — with thick boots and coarse hands. Estella would never look at me now, I thought. I would be too common for her.

"I won't be able to come any more," I told Miss Havisham on my next visit. "I have to start work."

"Estella is also leaving me," Miss Havisham told me. "She's going to France to finish her education. She must learn to be a grand lady."

Estella was prettier than ever, and still proud, but I felt she wore her pride like a veil, preventing the real Estella from shining through.

I often caught glimpses of her sweetness, even a sadness, that made me wish I could rescue her from her frozen tower.

"I am what Miss Havisham has made me," she confided one day. "I can't help being cold and hard. She never taught me to love. I wish I could."

I had wanted to tell her then that I loved her. My mind formed the words that were on the brink of my lips. Couldn't she feel it… couldn't she love me too? But before I could speak she had said quickly, as if she knew what I was thinking, "It's too late, Pip. I can't change myself now."

She had looked so unhappy that my heart felt wrenched in sympathy.

Now, on hearing Miss Havisham's words, my dream that we might one day be friends and equals had evaporated. Estella would be a grand lady, forever beyond my reach.

"I hope Estella will be very happy," I told Miss Havisham. "And you too."

"Huh!" she said, in disgust.

The next day, the lawyer, Mr. Jaggers, came unexpectedly to our house.

"You are fortunate, Pip," he exclaimed. "You are a man of great expectations!"

"What do you mean?" I gasped.

"I have been asked to tell you," he continued pompously, "that you now have a very large amount of money. Further," – he thrust out a restraining hand to stop my torrent of questions – "the person who has given you the money wants you to leave home, and come to London to learn how to be a gentleman."

He seemed to expand with each piece of news. "Furthermore," he concluded, "the name of this person is to remain a profound secret, until the person chooses to reveal it."

Joe and I looked at each other, completely amazed. "It must be Miss Havisham," I thought. "She's given me her fortune."

"If you have the slightest suspicion whom you think it might be, you are to keep your thoughts to yourself," said Mr. Jaggers, as if guessing my mind. "That is one condition of the gift."

"So – so you're going to London, Pip," Joe faltered. "You've been my best friend, and now you're going to be a grand gentleman. I'm very glad for you."

I was so excited I couldn't think about anything else. It never occurred to me that I might miss Joe. And I ignored the thought that Joe, now a lonely widower, might miss me.

"You need proper clothes before you come," advised Mr. Jaggers. "And they should not be the clothes of a working man. Go to the best tailor in town. Here's twenty guineas to begin with. And here's my card. Come to my London house in a week's time."

"Yes, sir," I replied, dreaming already of an elegant carriage and thoroughbred horse to carry me in style to my new life.

Chapter 4

An unwelcome visitor

I visited Mr. Trabb, the tailor. "I need a suit of fashionable clothes," I announced. "I can pay with cash."

"Don't hurt me by mentioning money," purred Mr. Trabb, flourishing rolls of fine cloth for my inspection.

I suddenly had a pleasant vision of my future. So this is what it was like to be rich. People would be so eager to please me!

A week later I went to Mr. Jaggers in London.

"Now, Pip," he told me. "You are to live with Mr. Herbert Pocket, a cousin of Miss Havisham. He will show you how to hold your knife and fork properly, how to dance, and how to choose wine. In short, he'll make a gentleman of you. Meanwhile the bank will put money in your account every week."

I listened greedily. I could think of no happier life.

"Ah! Here's my housekeeper with the coffee," he finished.

The housekeeper came in carrying a tray. I stared at her, with a shock of recognition. Surely I knew those eyes, that hair... Yet I couldn't think where I'd seen them before.

That afternoon I met Herbert Pocket, who was just my age. "We'll have such fun, Pip!" he cried. "We'll go to clubs and go racing!"

I could see my life was going to be even better than I'd imagined.

"I'm told you know Miss Havisham?" he commented. "Now there's a story!"

"What do you mean?" I asked.

"You don't know it?" said Herbert, astonished.

I shook my head. "I've always wanted to," I said eagerly.

"She was dressed for her wedding, a sumptuous feast laid on the table," Herbert began. "But as she was setting off to the church, her bridegroom ran away. Her life stopped at the moment of her ruined hopes."

"Poor Miss Havisham!" I said. "No wonder she's so sad. And how did Estella come in to her life?"

"She adopted her. No one knew where she came from. Miss Havisham brought her up to break men's hearts, just as hers was broken."

Life with Herbert was packed with amusement. I spent my huge allowance on clothes, good wine and entertainment.

"Why not learn to sail, Pip?" Herbert suggested one day.

I did, and liked it so much that I bought myself a fast boat to race against Herbert's yacht down the Thames.

Before long I was in debt, but I didn't care. Mr. Jaggers always gave me more money when I wanted it.

Joe came to visit me, wearing his shabby country clothes. He fidgeted uncomfortably as my servant let him in.

"You've gone right above me," he said. "London's no place for me. I won't bother you again."

I'm ashamed to say I was glad.

"Miss Havisham wants to see you," he told me, before he left.

I went back to the old house and found Miss Havisham, looking older, and Estella, returned for a while from France, now grown beautiful.

"Love her!" demanded Miss Havisham, playing with Estella's hair. "I adopted her to be loved!"

Silently, I repeated what I'd always known – I love her, I love her. I was amazed that I, once the blacksmith's boy, was destined for her.

"Real love…" mused Miss Havisham. "It's blind, unquestioning. It's humiliating, giving up your whole heart and soul!"

"I know!" I said aloud. "I do love you, Estella. I do!"

"You know that I have no heart," she replied, icy as winter. "I cannot love. I don't even love you, Miss Havisham."

Miss Havisham turned to me then. "What have I done?" she asked. "She's so hard… so cruel."

Estella was so cold and distant, I returned to my London apartment that evening filled with unhappiness. The night was wild and stormy and I came home as fast as I could. On my doorstep a strange man, old and tough-looking, was waiting for me.

"Who are you?" I asked, suspiciously.

"My, you've grown into a fine young gentleman," said the stranger. "Just what I hoped!"

"Y-you'd better come in," I stammered. Because I knew the man! Even though I couldn't recognize his features, I knew him, as though the wind and rain had blown away the years, and had swept us back to the churchyard where we had first met. It was Magwitch, the escaped prisoner.

Chapter 5

Secrets

Inside, to my horror, he hugged me. "You acted nobly, Pip. I never forgot."

"Don't!" I said. "It was nothing. I hope you are no longer a criminal. And now you must understand... Our ways are different... I can't ask you to stay —"

"Wait!" Magwitch ordered. "Didn't you guess where your money came from?"

"What?" I was astonished.

"I got away," Magwitch explained. "I went to Australia, and made a lot of money. I made it for you, Pip. Every penny I saved, I thought, this will help Pip, this will make a gentleman of him."

I was horrified. My money hadn't come from Miss Havisham after all, but from a man who had once been a criminal. It was tainted, dirty money!

"It was hard to come back, Pip," Magwitch continued. "I'm safe in Australia, but here my sentence still stands. If the police find me, I'll be hanged. But I wanted to see you. I wanted to see how my Pip had grown up."

I licked my lips nervously. "Why did you send me your money?"

A look of misery swept over his face. "I had a child once. A little girl. I lost her.

When I saw you on the marsh, you reminded me of her. She was the same age as you then."

"She died?" I queried.

"Who knows?" Magwitch wiped away tears. "I left her with her mother. Then I heard her mother was on trial for murder. God knows what happened to my little girl."

I couldn't help feeling disgusted. Magwitch and his family seemed like filthy rats from the gutter, without morality or decency.

"Don't sneer," Magwitch said. "Growing up isn't easy for poor folk. I've been in and out of jail all my life. I began as a child – begging, lying, thieving…"

He trailed off and looked at me pleadingly, wanting me to understand.

"You can stay here tonight," I muttered.

But I slept badly. Magwitch wasn't safe in England, and I didn't like him being here either.

Leaving him in my apartment the next morning, I went to see Mr. Jaggers.

"I know now where my money comes from," I told him.

"How?" he asked.

"Magwitch is here! He came to see me. And I want to know more."

Mr. Jaggers called his housekeeper to bring us coffee. As she came in, I was struck again by her likeness to someone I knew. This time I realized who it was. The way she held herself, her beauty, though faded now, was unmistakable. My jaw dropped open in amazement. This, surely, was Estella's mother!

Mr. Jaggers watched my face.

"You've guessed right," he said, when she'd left the room. "She is indeed Estella's mother. I was her lawyer when she was arrested for murder, and she was desperate about her daughter. I got her acquitted, but I took the child, and gave her to Miss Havisham, who wanted to adopt a little girl."

"Was it right to take the child from her mother?" I wondered, aloud.

Mr. Jaggers nodded with certainty. "I told her mother: 'If I get you off, I will save your child too.' Consider this, Pip. Estella's father was a criminal. I've seen pauper children of criminals grow up to meet the hangman themselves. Here was one pretty child out of the heap who could be saved."

"I understand. And her father? What happened to him? Who was he?"

Mr. Jaggers poured himself another drink. "Abel Magwitch," he said.

Chapter 6

Stormy seas and quiet waters

I was stunned.

"You must get him out of England as soon as you can," Mr. Jaggers went on. "He has plenty of enemies. If any of them knows he's here, they'll tell the police, and he'll end up dangling from a hangman's rope."

"I'll take him down the river as soon as the tide is right," I said. "Then I'll find a ship to take him to sea."

"One thing, Pip. Estella knows nothing about her parents. Nor does Miss Havisham. Promise you'll never tell."

I swore myself to secrecy. I'd do anything to protect my beautiful Estella.

The following fine night, Magwitch and I rowed down the Thames, past London Bridge, past the barges and oyster boats, until we reached the open sea.

Magwitch had agreed, for my sake, to leave the country. Now he sat back smiling, smoking his pipe.

"You know, Pip, dear boy," he said. "I'm happy. You've turned out well, and I'm still free."

He spoke too soon. Another vessel drew alongside in the dark, and a policeman leaped out into our boat.

"Abel Magwitch, I arrest you in the name of the law," he announced.

But Magwitch would not be taken so easily. As the policeman handcuffed him he fought back, then threw himself into the sea.

His eyes grew frantic with fright as he tried desperately to swim. He couldn't do it; his hands were chained behind his back. In an instant I jumped in after him. I had to save him! As I heaved his cold body inside the boat, the policeman looked down at us.

"If he ain't dead after tonight's activities, he'll get what he deserves when he comes before the judge!" he observed.

"He must go to hospital," I said firmly, and to my relief, this was allowed.

Magwitch was very ill. His time in the icy water, being half-drowned, was too much for his old heart. I stayed by his side every day. I realized how kind and true he'd been to me all these years. I wanted to do all I could in return.

"You've stuck by me, even though I'm under a dark cloud," he wheezed, coughing. His breath was very uneven. "I'm proud of you, Pip."

His voice grew fainter. "Dear boy," he managed to say. Then… silence.

I held his hand in mine. "You had a child once, whom you loved and lost. Can you understand what I say?"

He answered with a faint squeeze of my hand.

"She is alive and has good friends. She is a beautiful lady, and I love her."

With a last movement he raised my hand to his lips. Then a quiet look came into his eyes and his head rolled gently to one side.

Chapter 7

The heart of the fire

"You won't get Magwitch's money, now he's dead," Mr. Jaggers told me the next day. "Since he was an escaped criminal and died in England, the State owns everything he had."

I thought quickly. I had lived extravagantly and had large debts. I would have to earn my own way now. "I'll be a blacksmith after all," I announced. "I'm sure Joe will have me back."

Joe was as kind and generous as he'd always been. "It'll be like old times, you and me together, Pip," he smiled. "Just what I always wanted."

He never mentioned the time he'd come to London, when I hadn't been very welcoming. I saw now that Joe was the true gentleman, while I'd turned into a snob. I hated myself.

"Thank you, Joe," I said. "I'll never have a better friend than you."

I said goodbye to my friends in London, promising Herbert that I would write to him.

"Why don't you visit Miss Havisham again?" Joe asked. "It would be a friendly thing to do."

I thought he was right. I ought to.

She wept when I saw her, and sank on her knees. To see her thus, her white hair and worn face at my feet, shocked me.

"It's Estella!" she sobbed. "I've wronged her! I wanted to save her from a fate like mine," she went on. "I stole her heart and put ice in its place."

I knew that was true. She'd taken a happy little girl and made her into a copy of her own despair. I saw too that in shutting herself up, living in the past, she'd cut herself off from the healing influences of normal life. Her whole mind had grown diseased.

"Oh Pip!" she wept. "What have I done?"

I tried to comfort her.

Finally I left her, and gave a last glance at the dark room. I had a strange feeling I'd never return.

In that second I saw a candle tumble from its candlestick and fall onto Miss Havisham's dress. Instantly, faster than my dash to extinguish it, a great flame leaped up as she ran at me, shrieking. A whirl of fire blazed all around her and soared to the ceiling, lighting the crumbling wedding feast, the cobwebs and candelabra, in an intense red and orange light.

I took her in my arms and swept her outside, watching in horror as flames licked my arms, too. Scraps of tinder, that a moment ago had been her faded bridal dress, floated in the smoky air and fell in a black shower. I carried her into the garden and wrapped her in my coat to smother the flames, all the while calling for help.

I tried to ignore the searing pain where the flames had caught me, too. And behind me, the fire devoured the house.

At last, a doctor came. She began to speak as he tended to her, and I bent over her to catch her low and wandering voice.

"When the child first came, I meant to save her from misery like mine."

And then:

"Forgive me..."

After that, the world around me turned dark, and I felt and heard nothing.

I woke some weeks later, in my old bed at Joe's house.

"You've been very ill, Pip," Joe said, spooning medicine into my mouth. "You were badly burned in that fire."

"Miss Havisham?" I asked. "How is she?"

"I'm afraid she's dead, Pip," he replied gently.

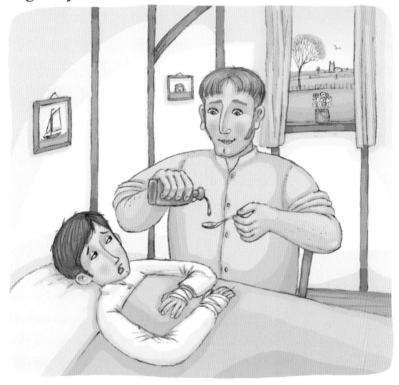

As soon as I felt stronger, I walked to the ruins of Miss Havisham's house. A cold silvery mist hid the blackened stones. As I came nearer, I saw a woman approach me.

"Estella!" I cried.

She seemed tired, her face pale and drawn, with a look I had never seen before… a saddened, softened light in those once proud eyes.

"I came back from France as soon as I heard of her death," she said. "Poor Miss Havisham! I thought of you often, Pip. You were kind to her."

"I was fond of her. She was unhappy," I replied.

"I'm going to sell the land," she went on. "It will be built on. Something else will take the place of that unhappy house..."

"Estella…" I interrupted.

She looked up at me. She seemed unsure of herself. "Tell me we are friends," she whispered.

"We will always be friends. I've always loved you," I said, reaching out for her.

Hand in hand, we walked out of the ruins. The mist was rising. I saw no shadows before us, only the clear air, calm and still. I knew Estella and I would never be parted again.

Charles Dickens 1812-1870

Charles Dickens lived in
London, England, during
the reign of Queen Victoria.
When he was 12, he was
sent to work in a factory
for three months. Dickens
hated it and never forgot how
miserable life was for the poor.

Dickens wrote two endings for *Great Expectations*.
In his first version, Pip and Estella meet briefly in
London, and then part forever. On the advice of
a friend, Dickens re-wrote the ending to suggest
that Pip and Estella will always be together. The
second ending is the most popular one today.

Edited by Susanna Davidson
Series editor: Lesley Sims
Designed by Michelle Lawrence

First published in 2007 by Usborne Publishing Ltd., Usborne House,
83-85 Saffron Hill, London EC1N 8RT, England. www.usborne.com
Copyright © 2007 Usborne Publishing Ltd.